Baby Beats

KAREN BLAIR

WALKER BOOKS
AND SUBSIDIARIES
LONDON · BOSTON · SYDNEY · AUCKLAND

Let's play music,
make a beat.

Clap your hands
and stamp your feet.

Beat the drums.
Boom, boom, bash.

Bang the cymbals.
Clash, clash, clash.

Tap your sticks.
Tock, tock, tick.

Shake the shakers.
Chick, chick, chick.

Strum, strum, strum
on your guitar.

Sing out loud.
La, la, la!

Sh, sh, sh.
Can you hear?

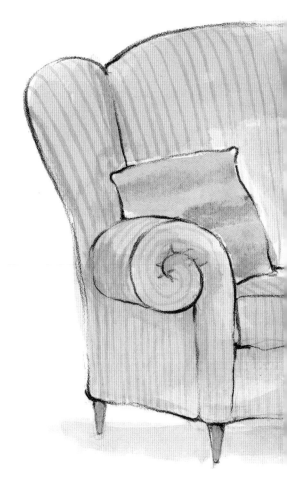

Someone's making music near.

Tinkle, *tinkle* his bell rings.

Miaow, miaow – and he sings!

Let's all play
and let's all sing!

Let's all dance
and sway and swing!

Music is just so much fun.

Sleep time now, the day is done.